Can I help, Mommy?

p

flip!

flap!

flip!

It was a good day to dry some laundry.
The sun was shining and the wind was blowing.

Bunny was helping his Mommy
by hanging the laundry on
the clothes line.

flap!

Suddenly the wind blew extra hard, and it whisked some of the laundry away.

whoosh!

whoosh!

whoosh!

"Come back!" cried Bunny, and he chased the laundry as it flipped and flapped off through the woods.

He found four noisy birds squabbling over his striped
socks. They wanted them to make cozy nests.

"I'll take those back, thank you!" cried Bunny.

Then Bunny saw
something moving
along the ground.

squeak!

"I'll take that back, thank you!" cried Bunny.

Then Bunny noticed the
corner of his baby brother's
special blanket poking out
from a hole in a tree.

He pulled as hard as he could, until out popped the blanket, and out popped a family of furry squirrels.

"I'll take that back, thank you!" cried Bunny.

Bunny gathered up all the laundry in the woods, until he had a big wobbly pile.

flip!

flap!

flip!

flap!

He took it all home and he hung it back on the clothes line.
It was hard work for a little bunny.

When Mommy came outside,
all the laundry was dry.